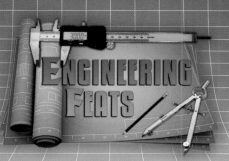

Virginia-class Submarines

Earle Rice Jr.

Mitchell Lane
PUBLISHERS

2001 SW 31st Avenue
Hallandale, FL 33009
www.mitchelllane.com

Mitchell Lane
PUBLISHERS

Printing   1   2   3   4   5   6   7   8

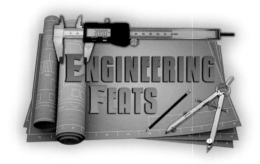

Designer: Sharon Beck
Editor: Jim Whiting

Library of Congress Cataloging-in-Publication Data
Names: Rice, Earle, author.
Title: The Virginia-class submarines / by Earle Rice Jr.
Description: Hallandale, FL : Mitchell Lane Publishers, 2018. | Series: Engineering feats | Includes
    bibliographical references and index. | Audience: Age 4-6
Identifiers: LCCN 2017046706 | ISBN 9781680201741 (library bound)
Subjects: LCSH: Virginia Class (Submarines)—Juvenile literature. | Nuclear submarines—United
    States—Juvenile literature.
Classification: LCC V858 .R53 2018 | DDC 623.825/74—dc23
LC record available at https://lccn.loc.gov/2017046706

eBook ISBN: 9-781-68020-175-8

PHOTO CREDITS: Design elements—RED_SPY/Getty Images, Ifness/Getty Images, Madmaxer/Getty Images, chictype/Getty Images, Thissatan/Getty Images, Nongkran_ch/Getty Images. Back cover photos (left to right)—NASA/JPL, Imagine China/Newscom, Henryk Sadura/Getty Images, NASA, Rehman/cc by-sa 2.0, U.S. Navy/Mass Communication Specialist Seaman Casey Hopkins/Public domain. Cover, p. 1—U.S. Navy photo by Mass Communication Specialist Seaman Casey Hopkins/Released; p. 5—PJF Military Collection/Alamy Stock Photo; p. 6—U.S. D.O.D. graphic by Ron Stern; p. 7—Louvre Museum/Seized during the French Revolution, Yuppi666/GFDL/cc-by-sa 3.0; p. 8—Geni/GFDL/cc-by-sa 4.0, OAR/National Undersea Research Program (NURP); p. 9—Ji-Elle/Public domain, Library of Congress; p. 10—Conrad Wise Chapman/American Civil War Museum; pp. 10, 11—Public domain; p. 13—Don S. Montgomery, U.S. Navy/, U.S. Navy photo NH 53787, U.S. Navy; p. 14—(top) en:User:XLerate/GFDL/cc-by-sa 3.9, (bottom)—Kayau/cc-by-sa 3.9; pp. 16, 17, 22, 26, 34-35, 36-37, 48—U.S. Navy Photo/Public domain; p. 17—US Navy photo courtesy of US Naval Historical Center; p. 19—U.S. Navy photo by Logistics Specialist 2nd Class Raymond Solis, Photo By: Mass Communication Specialist 1st Class Abraham Essenmacher/USPACOM; p. 21—U.S. Navy photo by Wendy Hallmark; p. 23—Courtesy of chinfo.navy.mil; p. 25—U.S. Navy photo by Mass Communication Specialist 1st Class Todd A. Schaffer, Lawlor/Released; p. 26—U.S. Navy photo by Journalist 1st Class James Pinsky; p. 27—U.S. Navy photo courtesy of Newport News Shipbuilding/Released, Ozma1981/cc-by-sa 3.0; p. 28—U.S. Navy photo by Photographer's Mate 1st Class David A. Levy; p. 29—U.S. Navy photo by Mass Communication Specialist 1st Class Todd A. Schaffer, Life of Riley/cc-by-sa 3.0; p. 30—U.S. Navy, Chief Photographer's Mate John E. Gay; p. 31—Sparkygravity/cc-by-sa 3.0; p. 33—APFootage/Alamy Stock Photo, U.S. Navy photo courtesy of General Dynamics/Released; p. 39—PJF Military Collection/Alamy Stock Photo.

CONTENTS

Words in **bold** throughout can be found in the Glossary.

1

"An Effort of Genius"

The christening of the USS *Indiana* (SSN-789) on April 29, 2017 was a celebration of the shipbuilder's art. Diane Donald executed an age-old ritual at the shipyards of Huntington Ingalls Industries, in Hampton Roads, Virginia. With one sure swing, she shattered a bottle of sparkling wine across the bow of the 16th *Virginia*-class submarine.

Diane Donald is the wife of retired Admiral Kirkland Donald, the former director of the Naval Nuclear Propulsion Program. To mark the occasion, she said, "It's the honor of a lifetime to be here today. While the size of the submarine alone is stunning, the complexity inside sets it apart from any other machine ever built. These ships are second to none, made in America by truly remarkable Americans."[1]

With the completion of the time-honored rite, *Indiana* entered service as one of the U.S. Navy's most advanced nuclear-powered fast attack submarines. *Virginia*-class submarines are designed for a wide range of missions, both in the open seas and close to shore. They were developed to replace the retiring *Los Angeles*-class submarines.

Virginia-class submarines feature dozens of new state-of-the-art technologies. Engineering advances increase their firepower, stealth, and handling ability. These **enhancements** elevate their warfighting capability to another level. They can reach submerged speeds greater

CHRISTENING OF

INDIANA

SSN 789

NEWPORT NEWS SHIPBUILDING
APRIL 29, 2017

Diane Donald, sponsor of the USS *Indiana* (SSN-789), stands behind a spray of sparkling wine as she christens the *Virginia*-class fast attack submarine. Witnesses look on approvingly, from left, Vice President Mike Pence, *Indiana*'s commanding officer Commander Jesse Zimbauer, and Newport News Shipbuilding President Matt Mulherin.

than 25 knots (29 miles/hour). And they can support multiple missions while remaining submerged for months at a time.

In short, *Virginia*-class submarines represent the very best undersea craft that American design, engineering, and shipbuilding expertise can produce. As Diane Donald put it, they are "second to none." They are also the product of centuries of development.

An artist's concept of a new *Virginia*-class fast attack submarine unleashing a torpedo. General Dynamics Electric Boat in Groton, Connecticut, and Newport News Shipbuilding in Newport News, Virginia, share construction of these new submarines. They delivered the first boat of this class, USS *Virginia* (SSN-774), to the U.S. Navy in 2004.

The idea of a submarine is not a new one. **Archimedes**, an ancient Greek scientist, established the physical principles of submersion (the act of being held completely under water or liquid for a long time) in the third century BCE (BEFORE COMMON ERA). Many people attempted to apply those principles over the following centuries for war, for exploration, and for fun.

Sculptor Simon-Louis Boquet's statue of Archimedes can be viewed in the Louvre Museum in Paris, France.

Gravity

m_{object}
(mass of the object)

ρ_{object} (density of the object)

ρ_{fluid}
(density of the fluid)

Buoyancy

FAST FACT

Archimedes defined the law of buoyancy: any object that is completely or partially submerged in a fluid at rest is acted upon by an upward force. The amount of that force is equal to the weight of the fluid displaced by the object.

A photograph of a full-sized model and a cutaway drawing of David Bushnell's submarine *Turtle*, which tried but failed to plant explosives on British ships in 1776. The model is displayed in the Royal Navy's submarine museum.

The first attempt by an American to develop a submersible craft for war fighting occurred in 1775, at the outset of the Revolutionary War. Connecticut farmer David Bushnell built a one-person diving chamber shaped like an egg. Called *Turtle*, it was hand-propelled and designed to slip submerged under the hull of an enemy ship and screw a time bomb to it. It would then withdraw to a safe distance before the bomb exploded. On three occasions the following year, *Turtle* failed to destroy British warships. Nevertheless, the attempts impressed George Washington, who commented, "I thought it was an effort of genius."[2]

American inventor Robert Fulton designed a larger and better hand-propelled submersible in 1800. He named it *Nautilus*. After failing

A full-sized model of Robert Fulton's submarine *Nautilus* can be seen at Cité de la Mer, Cherbourg, France. A cutaway view (top insert) shows the submarine's interior, and a full-sized section model (bottom insert) displays the sub's ribbed construction.

to sell it to France and England, he destroyed it. Fulton then turned his attention to inventing the steamboat, for which he received lasting fame.

During the American Civil War (1861–1865), both sides built submarines. The most famous was the Confederate submarine *H. L. Hunley*. It was a 40-foot steel submersible craft. *Hunley* succeeded in sinking the Union sloop *Housatonic* in Charleston harbor, South Carolina, with an

In this 1864 painting by Conrad Wise Chapman, titled *H. L. Hunley*, the artist portrays the inventor leaning against the submarine named for its creator. The submarine, often referred to simply as *Hunley*, belonged to the small navy of the Confederate States of America (CSA). As the first combat submarine to sink a warship, it played a small part in the American Civil War. Initially, *Hunley*'s supporters believed it would add a lethal weapon to the CSA's arsenal. But the ill-fated submarine soon demonstrated the inherent dangers of warfare beneath the surface of the sea. It sank on each of its first two trial runs, killing all aboard. Raised each time, it attacked and sank the USS *Housatonic*, a U.S. Navy sloop of war, in the outer harbor of Charleston, South Carolina. *Hunley* sank for a third and final time during the action, killing its eight crew members.

John Philip Holland looks skyward from the hatch of his submarine.

FAST FACT ✏

John Philip Holland founded the Electric Boat Company in 1899. He developed the first submarine to be formally commissioned in the U.S. Navy.

explosive. But it was caught in the blast and sank with all eight crew members on board.

In the years following the Civil War, inventor John Philip Holland made great advances in the design of submarines. He pioneered American efforts to combine the gasoline engine, which powered surface cruising, with a storage battery to propel the electric motors used for undersea propulsion. The U.S. submarine *Holland* (SS-1), named for him, served for several years as a test vehicle for systems used on many other American submarines in the process of development.

German designer Rudolph Diesel invented a heavy-oil engine for use in submarines in 1895. Germany's diesel-powered U-boats (from the German word *unterseebooten*, or undersea boats) became the scourge of Allied shipping during World War I (1914–1918). The submarine entered the modern arsenal of naval weaponry.

If George Washington were alive today, he would likely not hesitate to call the modern submarine "an effort of genius."

2
Yesterday and Today

"*Take her down!*"[1] shouted Commander Howard Gilmore on the night of February 7, 1943. Gilmore was the captain of the U.S. submarine *Growler*. It was his last command to the members of his crew. His final words would become forever etched in the annals of submarine lore.

On that night, *Growler* was in the western Pacific on its fourth war patrol. It was running on the surface to attack a Japanese convoy. Suddenly the Japanese gunboat *Hayasaki* appeared out of the darkness. It headed straight at *Growler* to ram and sink her. Gilmore sounded the collision alarm. "Left full rudder!"[2] he commanded, attempting to avoid the collision. But it was too late. His submarine rammed the gunboat amidships.

Growler tilted 50 degrees from the impact. Machine-gun fire from *Hayasaki* sprayed *Growler*'s conning tower. It killed a deck officer and a lookout and wounded Gilmore. He shouted, "Clear the bridge!"[3] An officer and three enlisted men scrambled into the open hatch and down the ladder. *Growler*'s executive officer, Arnold F. Schade, waited at the bottom for Gilmore to follow. On the bridge, Gilmore clung to its frame and shouted his legendary words.

Schade hesitated for a moment, trying to decide if he should save the ship or save the captain. He decided to obey Gilmore's last command to take *Growler* down. Though severely damaged, *Growler* limped back to port in Australia without her skipper. The Japanese

The Navy wasted little time in building upon *Nautilus*'s capabilities. It commissioned the world's first nuclear-powered ballistic submarine on December 30, 1959—USS *George Washington* (SSBN-598). The SSBN designator stands for Ship Submersible Ballistic Nuclear. "Nuclear" refers to the ship's propulsive power. *George Washington* was the first of five submarines of the class that bore its name.

The *George Washington*-class submarines were fitted with six torpedo tubes and sixteen tubes for Polaris missiles. These strategic nuclear missiles could be launched while the sub was submerged. This capability greatly increased its chances of remaining undetected before firing. Earlier diesel subs carried strategic ballistic missiles, but they were cruise missiles and required the submarine to surface so it could launch them. With the addition of Polaris missiles, submarines completed the third arm of the U.S. nuclear triad. Nuclear **ordnance** could henceforth be delivered in three ways—via land-based intercontinental ballistic missiles (ICBMs), aircraft (B-52 bombers), and submerged submarines. Beginning in 1981, The *George Washington*-class subs were replaced by *Ohio*-class vessels.

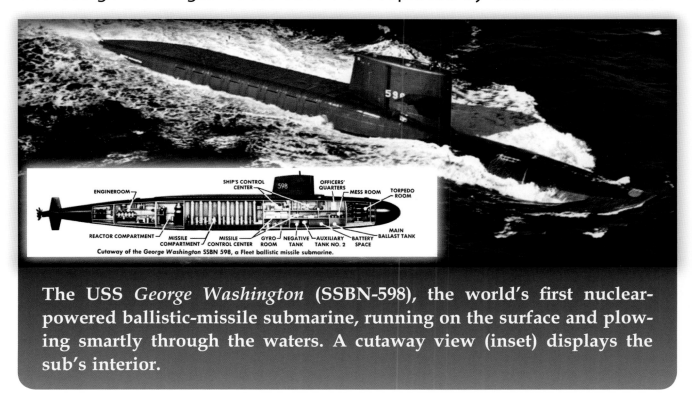

The USS *George Washington* (SSBN-598), the world's first nuclear-powered ballistic-missile submarine, running on the surface and plowing smartly through the waters. A cutaway view (inset) displays the sub's interior.

3

The Name of the Game

On April 25, 2017, the guided-missile submarine USS *Michigan* (SSGN-727) put in at the South Korean port of Busan. The Navy called it a routine visit. In reality, its presence represented a show of force. It hardly seemed a coincidence that it arrived on the 85th anniversary of the birth of North Korea's army. The celebration to the north was huge and threatening. At the same time, U.S. and South Korean forces were preparing for a joint military exercise.

At the U.S. Army's garrison in Seoul, reporters asked General Vincent Brooks, commander of U.S. forces in South Korea, if *Michigan*'s arrival was meant to send a message to the North Koreans. Brooks replied, "We're ready, and we are committed to the (South Korea)-U.S. alliance."[1] *Michigan*'s timely arrival represented a solid display of American commitment.

The U.S. Navy's modern undersea fleet consists of three basic types: ballistic missile submarines (known as boomers), guided missile submarines, and attack submarines. All are nuclear-powered.

Fourteen *Ohio*-class vessels are ballistic submarines (SSBNs). They are armed with up to 24 Trident II submarine-launched ballistic missiles (SLBMs), and four Mark 48 torpedo tubes for self-defense. Their mission is not to hunt and destroy enemy ships and submarines. Their task is simply to run silently (under nuclear propulsion), avoid

The USS *Michigan* (SSGN-727), an *Ohio*-class guided-missile submarine, arriving in Busan, South Korea, for a routine port visit on December 24, 2010. Homeported in Bangor, Washington, *Michigan* is deployed to the U.S. 7th Fleet's area of responsibility. A Republic of Korea Navy band (inset) greets *Michigan* as it arrives for another port visit to Busan on June 23, 2015.

detection, and provide the ever-present threat of an unstoppable nuclear response.

Four additional *Ohio*-class submarines are designated SSGN, which stands for Submersible Ship Guided (missile) Nuclear. They carry as many as 154 Tomahawk cruise missiles (SLCMs). They also carry Harpoon missiles fired through the sub's four torpedo tubes. Guided-missile subs provide conventional warfare capabilities. The *Michigan* belongs to this class.

Attack submarines are designated SSN, for Submersible Ship Nuclear. They are usually armed with guided missiles and torpedoes. They perform a variety of vital national security missions, which come directly from the National Command Authority. They also come from Fleet and Unified Commanders and Carrier Battle Group Commanders.[3] Mission assignments include:

- **Intelligence**, **Surveillance**, and **Reconnaissance** (ISR)
- Precision Tomahawk strikes
- Special Operating Forces (SOF) insertions
- Mine reconnaissance
- Offensive mining
- Antisurface and antisubmarine warfare[4]

The three classes of attack submarines currently in service are the *Seawolf*-class, *Los Angeles*-class, and *Virginia*-class. The Navy introduced

In November 2003, the U.S. submarine *Ohio* entered drydock at Puget Sound Naval Shipyard to begin a 36-month refueling and conversion overhaul. *Ohio* underwent a conversion from a ballistic missile submarine (SSBN) to a guided missile submarine (SSGN).

Los Angeles-class boats in 1976. They are often referred to as the "688 class" after the original *Los Angeles*'s designation of SSN-688. They were designed and built on lessons learned from the *Thresher/Permit*-class and the *Sturgeon*-class attack submarines of the Cold War era. Since then, the *Los Angeles*-class subs have made up the bulk of the Navy's attack submarines. They weigh 6,927 tons and are 360 feet (110 meters) long by 33 feet (10 meters) wide. Thirty-six were in service as of 2017. Another 26 have been retired.

FAST FACT

The film adaptation of Tom Clancy's *The Hunt for Red October* features the *Los Angeles*-class submarine USS *Dallas* (SSN-700). *Call of Duty*, the popular video game, uses USS *Chicago* (SSN-721) as a platform to launch a task force operation.

Technicians at Keyport, Washington, maintain a Mark 48 Advance Capability torpedo in 1982.

They feature better sound quieting and a larger propulsion system than earlier subs. Their armament consists of both Tomahawk and Harpoon missiles. They also carry Mark 48 torpedoes for four torpedo tubes.

The final 23 boats (SSNs 751–773) are even quieter and incorporate an advanced **sonar** suite combat system. Designated as the 688I class (I for improved), they are equipped with 12 vertical launch tubes for Tomahawk missiles. Also, the diving planes were shifted from the sail to the bow to enable under-ice operations, which need a strengthened sail for breaking ice.

Los Angeles-class submarines have a nominal service life of 33 years.[5] Thus, they are all either approaching retirement or have reached it. The Navy began planning their replacement in 1983. At that time the United States was still engaged in the Cold War with the Soviet Union. Navy designers set out to create a submarine large and strong enough to combat the threat posed by an increasing number of advanced Soviet ballistic and attack submarines. They designed the *Seawolf*-class to counter the Soviet threat.

At a length of 353 feet (108 meters), a beam of 40 feet (12 meters), and a surface weight of 8,600 tons, *Seawolf*-class submarines are larger than their *Los Angeles*-class predecessors. They are also quieter, faster, more heavily armed, and more technologically advanced. But these

Seawolf (SSN-21), the first of three boats in its class, undergoes construction at the Electric Boat Division of General Dynamics in Groton, Connecticut. Margaret Dalton, spouse of Secretary of the Navy John H. Dalton, christened *Seawolf* on June 24, 1995.

advancements came at a high cost—each submarine cost $300 to $350 billion to build.

The Navy planned to construct 12 *Seawolf* boats at a total projected cost of $33.6 billion. But when the Cold War ended in 1991, production on the program ended. Only three boats were built. The cancellation still left the Navy with a need for a new, cheaper class of submarines to replace the *Los Angeles*-class boats.

In February, 1991, the Navy initiated a development study under the codename Centurion. The *Virginia*-class submarines were born from that study. They became the first U.S. Navy warships designed using computer-aided design (CAD) and visualization. As work progressed, high-technology advances became the name of the game.

4
Integration and Innovation

The *Virginia*-class attack submarine is an advanced stealth multi-mission vessel, designed for both deep ocean antisubmarine warfare and shallow water operations. *Virginia*-class submarines are the Navy's newest, fastest, and quietest submarines. And they are extremely efficient.

"We are able to make our own water. We make our own oxygen. We have a sustained fuel source in our nuclear reactor," said Captain Dan Reiss, skipper of the *Virginia*-class submarine *New Mexico* (SSN-779). "So the one thing we have to come in and out for is food and the cooks in the galley make some incredible meals, given the space they have to work."[1]

Thirteen *Virginia*-class submarines are currently in service. Fifteen more are either under construction or under contract. Two are built every year at a cost of $2 billion each. "The United States, through our submarine force for nearly a hundred years now, has gained and maintained a strong undersea advantage,"[2] says Captain Brian Sittlow. He leads a squadron of submarines from the Naval Submarine Base New London at Groton, Connecticut. The addition of *Virginia*-class submarines will help preserve that advantage for many years to come.

Virginia-class fast attack submarines are the most advanced submarines in the world. They are built by a shipbuilding team consisting of the Electric Boat Division of General Dynamics and the Newport News Shipbuilding Division of Huntington Ingalls Industries. These

Crewmembers stand in ranks topside aboard the *Virginia*-class fast attack submarine *New Mexico* (SSN-779) during a commissioning ceremony practice at Naval Station Norfolk. Her commissioning took place on March 21, 2010. Admiral Jonathan Greenert (inset), Chief of Naval Operations (CNO), meets *New Mexico*'s crew and tours the submarine's compartments. During certification tests, the new submarine performed various tracking, deter-

shipyards are located in Groton, Connecticut, and Newport News, Virginia, respectively.

Electric Boat is the lead design authority on the program. By 2007, the team had spent around 35 million labor hours designing *Virginia*-class boats. It builds the pressure hull, engine room, and control room. Newport News builds the stern, **habitability** and machinery spaces, torpedo room, sail, and bow. The two yards alternate work on the reactor plant.

The USS *Virginia* (SSN-774), the first of a new class of fast attack submarines, undergoes construction at Electric Boat Company of Groton, Connecticut. Electric Boat is the lead design authority for the new attack submarines. A new Caterpillar 3512B V-12 twin-turbo charged diesel engine generates *Virginia*'s onboard power requirements. A liquid crystal display (LCD) (inset), visible to many eyes, monitors all of the engine's readings.

FAST FACT ✎

Upwards of 10,000 workers at Electric Boat and Newport News build each frame and compartment of *Virginia*-class submarines. Five thousand vendors across all 50 states supply millions of individual parts.[3]

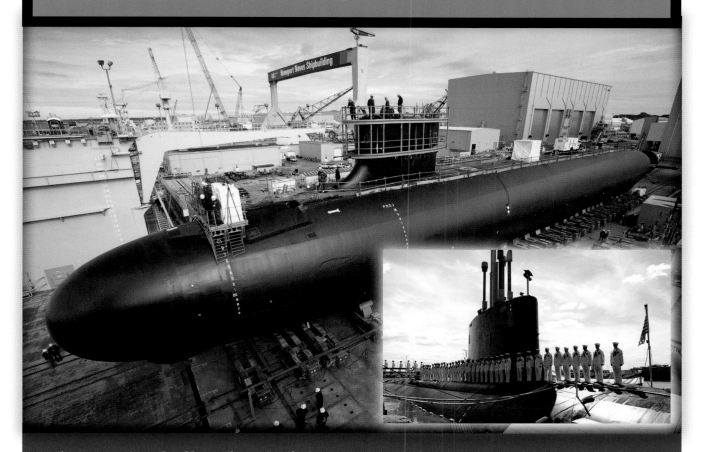

The massive hull and sail of the *Virginia*-class submarine USS *Minnesota* (SSN-783) dwarfs the humans on and nearby the boat during its construction at Newport News Shipbuilding. *Minnesota*'s crew (inset) mans the sub during its commissioning at Naval Base Norfolk on September 7, 2013.

They also alternate final assembly, testing, outfitting, and delivery. The construction and completion of each submarine requires about nine million labor hours.

Engineering teams and design-and-build teams at Electric Boat work together with the Naval Sea Systems Command. They are masters of design **innovation**. Computer-aided design and engineering (CAD/CAE) simulations help make the *Virginia*-class submarines the best they can be. General characteristics of this class are:

Length: 377 feet (115 meters)

Beam: 33 feet (10 meters)

Displacement: Approximately 7,800 tons (7,925 metric tons) submerged

Propulsion: One nuclear reactor, one shaft

Speed: 25+ knots (28+ miles/hour; 46+ kilometers/hour)

Crew: 132: 15 officers, 117 enlisted

Armament: Tomahawk missiles, 12 Vertical Launch System (VLS) tubes, MK48 Advanced Capability (ADCAP) torpedoes, four torpedo tubes[4]

Machinist's Mate 3rd Class Nicholas Thesing conducts a preload inspection of a torpedo tube aboard USS *Portsmouth* (SSN-707), a *Los Angeles*-class submarine.

FAST FACT

The torpedo room on *Virginia*-class boats can be made to house special operations forces. They exit the boat through a large lock-in/lock-out chamber while the submarine remains submerged. Older subs required surfacing.

In August 2011, a torpedo room weapons team prepares to receive a torpedo aboard the attack submarine USS *Albany* at Newport News shipyard. An inset shows a torpedo lodged in its tube and ready to fire.

Virginia-class submarines are built in Blocks, which are numbered I–VII. Boats of Blocks I and II have been completed and are in service. Block III boats are either in service, recently launched, or still under construction. Boats of Block IV are either under construction or on order. Blocks V–VII boats are still in the planning stage.

All of the boats are built in **modules**. This method allows large segments of equipment to be built outside the hull. These segments are called "rafts." The rafts are then inserted into sections of the pressure hull. Block I boats were built in 10 sections. Boats of Block II and their successors have just four sections to cut costs.

Modular construction makes it easy to remove outdated equipment and insert newly designed upgrades as the technology progresses. **Integrated** enclosures to accept standard-size 19- and 24-inch equipment are fitted into the hull section. Command, Control, Communications, and Intelligence (C3I) systems cut costs by using commercial-off-the-shelf (COTS) instead of custom-made parts. Computer monitors feature touchscreens.

Modular isolated deck structures are inserted. For example, the boat's command center is installed as a single unit resting on cushioned mounts. A four-button, two-axis joy stick controls the boat's fly-by-wire steering

Control room of the fast attack submarine USS *Seawolf* (SSN-21). Personnel, with all eyes glued to their display monitors, man the underway control watch.

and diving. A rudder in the stern controls left and right movement; diving planes in the bow turn the sub up or down.

The boats are driven mostly through software codes and electronics. This frees an operator from having to manually control every movement. "This allows you the flexibility to be in **littorals** [coastal regions] or periscope depth for extended periods of time without being detected,"[5] said former program manager Captain David Goggins.

General Electric provides the boat's main propulsion units. Its S9G pressure water reactor is designed to last for the lifetime of the submarine. Two turbine engines with one shaft and a United Defense pump jet propulsor generate 29.84 **megawatts** of power.

The boat's sail (formerly referred to as the conning tower) contains eight unified masts for the first time. The Universal Modular Mast (UMM) houses a snorkel mast, two **photonic** masts, two tactical communications masts, one or two high-data-rate satellite communication masts, a radar mast, and an electronic warfare mast. These submarines no longer need a periscope. Instead, color, black-and-white, and infrared cameras imbedded in the photonics masts send visual images to the control room. Signal data is also received and processed from its spherical bow sonar **array**, dual towed arrays, and flank array suite. A single *Virginia*-class sub possesses more signal processing power than yesterday's entire submarine fleet combined.[6]

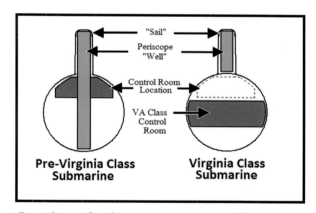

Sectional views compare the design of a *Virginia*-class submarine using a photonics mast with that of earlier submarines fitted with periscopes.

The Navy expects *Virginia*-class submarines to remain in service past 2060. With the aid of integration and innovation, they may be able to extend their service life until 2070 or even longer.

5

Block III and Beyond

The task of maintaining America's undersea edge never ends. Ten boats of Blocks I and II of the *Virginia*-class advanced attack submarines are in service. Another eight boats of Block III are in service or soon to become operational. Each Block introduces new advances in engineering and technology. And each improvement helps to keep America's submarine fleet ahead of its would-be adversaries.

In August 2014, the Navy accepted delivery of USS *North Dakota*, the first of the Block III submarines. Block III subs have two major enhancements.

One is a Large Aperture Bow (LAB) array which replaces the spherical sonar array in the bow of the boat. "The LAB array provides improved passive listening capabilities over traditional spherical arrays employed on earlier submarines," noted Rear Admiral Joseph Tofalo, director of undersea warfare. "The LAB array includes a medium-frequency active array. The **hydrophones** used to determine a bearing of either incoming passive sounds or active reflected sounds are taken directly from previous design and technology advancements."[1]

The other new development is the Virginia Payload Tubes (VPTs). They replace twelve individual 21-inch (53 centimeters) diameter vertical launch system (VLS) tubes for Tomahawk cruise missiles. The VPTs consist of two larger 87-inch (221 centimeters) diameter tubes

told, each Block V sub will be able to fire off 40 Tomahawk missiles. The increased armament will triple the number of shore targets that Block V boats can cover.

Even though VPM's are designed primarily for Tomahawk missiles, they are being engineered to accept new payloads as they are developed.

A tactical Block IV Tomahawk cruise missile built by Raytheon.

"You build a very flexible host platform," claims Admiral David Johnson, program executive officer.[5]

In addition to improvements with each successive Block, the Navy also upgrades every attack and guided missile submarine every four to six years under a program called Submarine Warfare Federated Tactical Systems (SWFTS). Electronics, sensors, combat control systems, and imaging systems are examined and replaced as needed. Ballistic-missile submarines will be similarly upgraded in the future. SWFTS upgrades provide another way to keep the Navy's undersea fleet at the cutting edge of technology.

As of 2017, Blocks VI and VII are planned to add another five boats each to the *Virginia*-class fleet. Some sources believe they will not be necessary, saying that such a long production run would be unusual. Time will tell.

The ever-evolving *Virginia*-class submarines represent masterpieces of the engineering art and hands-on craftsmanship. They are expected to serve well into the latter half of this century. In time, however, even these technological masterworks will need replacing. Unsurprisingly, their replacement is already in the works.

In 2014, Navy engineers started initial preparatory work on the advanced fast attack submarine of the future. Designated SSN(X), the future submarine might dispense with noise-making moving parts, such as a propulsor and its driveshaft. Some other projected features include making it a mothership for unmanned underwater vehicles

FAST FACT

Naval engineers would like to develop a nature-inspired biomimetic propulsor system that would eliminate the noise-making driveshaft and spinning propulsor. The concept, which would mark a great leap forward, has so far eluded them.

At the Battleship Oregon Memorial at Governor Tom McCall Waterfront Park in Portland, Oregon, Secretary of the Navy Ray Mabus unveils a depiction of the future *Virginia*-class submarine USS *Oregon* (SSN-793). Portland Mayor Charles Hale looks on.

(UUVs). In this scenario, the submarine would function as an underwater aircraft carrier. A torpedo-propulsion design from Pennsylvania State University indicates that remotely controlled torpedoes with a range of 200 nautical miles (230 miles/370 kilometers) are possible.

Whatever advances the future may hold, Americans can rest assured that *Virginia*-class submarines will rule supreme under the deep blue seas for decades to come.

☆ The Electric Boat division of General Dynamics and the Newport News Shipbuilding division of Huntington Ingalls are the only two U.S. shipyards capable of building nuclear submarines.

☆ USS *John Warner* (SSN-785) is the first *Virginia*-class submarine named for a person—in this case, former Virginia Senator John Warner. All others currently in service are named for U.S. states.

☆ USS *Hyman G. Rickover*, currently on order, will be the second *Virginia*-class submarine named for a person. It is named for the late Admiral Hyman G. Rickover, known as the "Father of the Nuclear Navy."

☆ USS *Indiana* (SSN-789) is the third U.S. Navy ship with that name. The first was a battleship (BB 1) that helped to blockade Cuba during the Spanish-American War (1898). The second, also a battleship (BB 58), earned nine battle stars in the Pacific Theater during World War II.

☆ New technologies have reduced the number of crew watchstanders onboard *Virginia*-class submarines by 15 as compared to *Seawolf*-class subs.

☆ Three-dimensional computer-aided design (CAD) on the program totally replaced engineering paper drawings and wooden mock-ups of the past.

☆ The U.S. Navy only accepts volunteers in the submarine service. Volunteers must first undergo rigorous testing and observation due to the stressful nature of the duty.

QUICK STATS

★ Maximum diving depth of *Virginia*-class submarines exceeds 800 feet (240 meters) and possibly extends to about 1,600 feet (490 meters).

★ The submarine's lock-in/lock-out chamber is large enough to host a nine-man Special Operations Team. It was designed to hold a since-abandoned Advanced SEAL Delivery System (ASDS), that is, a midget submarine.

★ It costs $50 million a year to operate a single *Virginia*-class submarine.

★ Mark 60 CAPTOR mines (enCAPsulated TORpedo) may be included in the boat's armament. It is the only deep-water, antisubmarine naval mine in the U.S. arsenal.

★ Boats can deploy a Long-term Mine Reconnaissance System (LMRS) to detect mine fields as much as 120 miles (200 kilometers) in advance of its path. It uses an unmanned underwater vehicle that is launched and retrieved through its torpedo tubes.

★ The sub's high-tech photonics system (that replaces the periscope) delivers real-time imaging on displays that more than one person can see.

★ Total cost of the *Virginia*-class submarine program is estimated at $92.55 billion, not including adjustments for price/inflation

★ The Navy redesigned about 20 percent of the submarine to reduce the cost of producing the Block III version.

★ The future submarine SSN(X) is currently projected to be authorized in 2034.

TIMELINE

1775 Colonist David Bushnell builds a one-person diving chamber called *Turtle*.

1800 Robert Fulton builds hand-propelled submersible named *Nautilus*.

1864 Confederate submarine *J. L. Hunley* sinks the Union sloop *Housatonic* in the harbor at Charleston, South Carolina, during the Civil War.

1895 German designer Rudolph Diesel invents a heavy-oil engine for use in submarines.

1899 John Philip Holland founds the Electric Boat Company.

1914–1918 German U-boats become the scourge of Allied shipping during World War I.

1943 Commander Howard Gilmore gives his life to save his submarine, USS *Growler*.

1954 The U.S. Navy enters the nuclear age with the commissioning of the USS *Nautilus* (SSN-571) on September 30.

1955 *Nautilus* puts to sea on January 17.

1958 *Nautilus* passes under the polar icecap in August.

1959 The U.S. Navy commissions USS *George Washington* (SSBN-598), the world's first nuclear-powered ballistic submarine.

1976 U.S. Navy introduces the *Los Angeles*-class submarines.

1981 *Ohio*-class submarines enter service in U.S. Navy.

1983 U.S. Navy begins planning the replacement of the *Los Angeles*-class submarines.

1991 Production ends on the *Seawolf*-class program. *Virginia*-class submarines emerge from Centurion study.

2007 Labor hours spent on designing *Virginia*-class boats reach 35 million.

2014 U.S. Navy accepts delivery of USS *North Dakota* (SSN-784), the first of the Block III submarines. Navy engineers start initial preparatory work on SSN(X), the advanced fast attack submarine of the future.

2017 USS *Michigan* (SSGN-727) puts in to the South Korean port of Busan on April 25. USS *Indiana* (SSN-789) is christened on April 29 in Hampton Roads, Virginia.

2019 Scheduled production date for Block V *Virginia*-class submarines.

2060–2070 Projected service life of *Virginia*-class submarines.

Chapter 1—"An Effort of Genius"

1. "Huntington Ingalls Industries Christians Virginia-Class Submarine Indiana at Newport News Shipbuilding." Huntington Ingalls Industries, Inc. April 29, 2017. https://globenewswire.com/news-release/2017/04/29/974813/0/en/VIDEO-RELEASE-Huntington-Ingalls-Industries-Christens-Virginia-Class-Submarine-Indiana-Newport-News-Shipbuilding.html

2. Clay Blair Jr., *Silent Victory: The U.S. Submarine War Against Japan* (Vol. 1. New York: J. B. Lippincott Company, 1975), p. 3.

Chapter 2—Yesterday and Today

1. Clay Blair Jr., *Silent Victory: The U.S. Submarine War Against Japan* (Vol. 1. New York: J. B. Lippincott Company, 1975), p. 348.

2. Ibid.

3. Ibid.

4. Ibid., p. xv.

5. Ibid.

6. "History of the USS Nautilus (SSN 571)." Submarine Force Museum. http://www.ussnautilus.org/nautilus/

Chapter 3—The Name of the Game

1. Kim Gamel, "US Sub Makes Port Call In South Korea Just In Time For North Korea Military Parade." *Stars and Stripes*. April 25, 2017. http://taskandpurpose.com/uss-michigan-submarine-north-korea

2. Sebastien Roblin, "Why Russia and China Fear America's Ohio-Class Submarines." *The National Interest*. May 14, 2017. http://nationalinterest.org/blog/the-buzz/why-russia-china-fear-americas-ohio-class-submarines-19120

3. *2008 Submarine Encyclopedia: U.S. Navy Forces Today and Tomorrow*. Three CD-Rom set. Washington, DC: Department of Defense, 2007, Disc 2.

4. Ibid.

5. "US Navy's Los Angeles-class submarine returns to fleet." Naval Today. April 14, 2017. http://navaltoday.com/2017/04/14/us-navys-los-angeles-class-submarine-returns-to-fleet/

Chapter 4—Integration and Innovation

1. "Navy's newest sub the USS New Mexico to be the fastest, quietest yet." CBS News. May 11, 2017. http://krqe.com/2017/05/10/navys-newest-submarine-to-be-the-fastest-and-quietest-yet/amp/

2. Ibid.

3. "The *Virginia*-Class: America's New Fast Attack Submarines." Huntington Ingalls. http://nns.huntingtoningalls.com/wp-content/uploads/2016/07/virginia-class-infographic.pdf

4. "Latest Virginia-Class Submarine Named." *The Maritime Executive*. May 24, 2015. http://www.maritime-executive.com/article/latest-virginia-class-submarine-named

5. Kris Osborn, "The Virginia-Class Submarine Is Arguably the Best in the World (And the U.S. Navy Wants More)." *The National Interest*. January 4, 2017. http://nationalinterest.org/blog/the-buzz/the-virginia-class-submarine-arguably-the-best-the-world-the-18941

6. "SSN-774 Virginia-class NSSN New Attack Submarine Centurion." Federation of American Scientists. https://fas.org/man/dod-101/sys/ship/nssn.htm

Chapter 5—Block III and Beyond

1. Kris Osborn, "Navy Receives First Block III Virginia-Class Submarine." *DoD Buzz*. September 4, 2014. https://www.dodbuzz.com/2014/09/04/navy-receives-first-block-iii-virginia-class-submarine/

2. Kris Osborn, "Navy Wants 28 More Tomahawks on Virginia-Class Submarines Sooner." Military.com. March 16, 2015. http://www.military.com/daily-news/2015/03/16/navy-wants-28-more-tomahawks-on-virginia-class-submarines-sooner.html

3. Dave Majumdar, "Navy: The Future of Virginia Class Submarines." *Scout*. September 27, 2016. http://www.scout.com/military/warrior/story/1711169-navy-the-future-of-virginia-class-submarines

4. Ibid.

5. Kris Osborn, "Navy Considers Future After Virginia-Class Subs." Defense Tech. February 12, 2014. https://www.defensetech.org/2014/02/12/navy-considers-future-after-virginia-class-subs

Doeden, Matt. *Submarines*. Pull Ahead Books. Minneapolis, MN: Lerner Publishing Group, 2005.

Kramer, Sydelle. *Submarines*. Step into Reading Series. New York: Random House Books for Young Readers, 2005.

Mallard, Neil. *Submarines*. Eyewitness Guides. New York: Dorling Kindersley Publishers, 2003.

Mattern, Joanne. *Submarines*. Rookie Read-About Science: How Things Work Series. New York: Children's Press/Franklin Watts Trade (Scholastic), 2015.

Murphy, Aaron. *What's Inside: Submarines*. What's Inside Series. New York: Sandy Creek Press/Barnes & Noble, 2014.

WORKS CONSULTED

2008 Submarine Encyclopedia: U.S. Navy Forces Today and Tomorrow. Three CD-Rom Set. Washington, DC: Department of Defense, 2007.

Blair, Clay, Jr. *Silent Victory: The U.S. Submarine War Against Japan*. Vols. 1 & 2. New York: J. B. Lippincott Company, 1975.

Gamel, Kim. "US Sub Makes Port Call In South Korea Just In Time For North Korea Military Parade." *Stars and Stripes*. April 25, 2017. http://taskandpurpose.com/uss-michigan-submarine-north-korea

"History of the USS Nautilus (SSN 571)." Submarine Force Museum. http://www.ussnautilus.org/nautilus/

"Huntington Ingalls Industries Christians Virginia-Class Submarine Indiana at Newport News Shipbuilding." Huntington Ingalls Industries, Inc. April 29, 2017. https://globenewswire.com/news-release/2017/04/29/974813/0/en/VIDEO-RELEASE-Huntington-Ingalls-Industries-Christens-Virginia-Class-Submarine-Indiana-Newport-News-Shipbuilding.html

"Latest Virginia-Class Submarine Named." *The Maritime Executive*. May 24, 2015. http://www.maritime-executive.com/article/latest-virginia-class-submarine-named

Majumdar, Dave. "Navy: The Future of Virginia Class Submarines." *Scout*. September 27, 2016. http://www.scout.com/military/warrior/story/1711169-navy-the-future-of-virginia-class-submarines

"Navy's newest sub the USS New Mexico to be the fastest, quietest yet." CBS News. May 11, 2017. http://krqe.com/2017/05/10/navys-newest-submarine-to-be-the-fastest-and-quietest-yet/amp/

Osborn, Kris. "The Virginia-Class Submarine Is Arguably the Best in the World (And the U.S. Navy Wants More)." *The National Interest*. January 4, 2017. http://nationalinterest.org/blog/the-buzz/the-virginia-class-submarine-arguably-the-best-the-world-the-18941

———. "Navy Wants 28 More Tomahawks on Virginia-Class Submarines Sooner." Military.com. March 16, 2015. http://www.military.com/daily-news/2015/03/16/navy-wants-28-more-tomahawks-on-virginia-class-submarines-sooner.html

———. "Navy Considers Future After Virginia-Class Subs." Defense Tech. February 12, 2014. https://www.defensetech.org/2014/02/12/navy-considers-future-after-virginia-class-subs

———. "Navy Receives First Block III Virginia-Class Submarine." *DoD Buzz*. September 4, 2014. https://www.dodbuzz.com/2014/09/04/navy-receives-first-block-iii-virginia-class-submarine/

Roblin, Sebastien. "Why Russia and China Fear America's Ohio-Class Submarines." *The National Interest*. May 14, 2017. http://nationalinterest.org/blog/the-buzz/why-russia-china-fear-americas-ohio-class-submarines-19120

"SSN-774 Virginia-class NSSN New Attack Submarine Centurion." Federation of American Scientists. https://fas.org/man/dod-101/sys/ship/nssn.htm

"The *Virginia*-Class: America's New Fast Attack Submarines." Huntington Ingalls. http://nns.huntingtoningalls.com/wp-content/uploads/2016/07/virginia-class-infographic.pdf

"US Navy's Los Angeles-class submarine returns to fleet." Naval Today. April 14, 2017. http://navaltoday.com/2017/04/14/us-navys-los-angeles-class-submarine-returns-to-fleet/

ON THE INTERNET

"History Fun for Kids." Go-Parts. https://www.go-parts.com/article-under-the-sea-history-of-submarines.html

"Spies of the Sea – Submarines." Kinoose Learning, September 30, 2013. http://kinooze.com/spies-of-the-sea-submarines/

"Submarine Facts for Kids." Science Kids. http://www.sciencekids.co.nz/sciencefacts/vehicles/submarines.html

Archimedes (ahr-kuh-MEE-dez)—ancient Greek inventor and mathematician (c.290–212 BCE); discoverer of the law of buoyancy

array (uh-RAY)—device which provides sonar sensor input to a submarine's combat system

biomimetics (bye-oh-meh-ME-tiks)—the young science of adapting designs from nature to solve modern problems

commissioning (kuh-MISH-shun-ing)—formally committing a naval vessel to service

deployment (di-PLOI-ment)—the act of spreading out, or bringing or coming into action systematically, especially strategically

enhancement (en-HANS-ment)—the act of increasing the attractiveness or other quality of a person, place, or thing

habitability (hab-i-tuh-BIL-i-tee)—suitability for living in or on

hydrophone (HIE-droh-fohn)—a device for listening under water

inherent (in-HER-ent)—existing in something as a natural or permanent characteristic or quality

innovation (in-oh-VAY-shun)—introduction of a new process or way of doing things

integrate (IN-teh-grayt)—to combine or form a part or parts into a whole

intelligence (in-TEL-i-jehns)—information, news, especially that of military value

littoral (LI-tuh-rehl)—a coastal region

megawatt (MEG-uh-waht)—one million watts

module (MAH-jool)—an independent unit in a building, spacecraft, submarine, etc.

ordnance (ORD-nans)—military supplies, especially weapons and their equipment and ammunition

photonics (foh-TOHN-niks)—the use of photons to transmit information

reconnaissance (ri-KON-uh-sahns)—an exploration or examination of an area in order to obtain information about it, especially for military purposes

sonar (SOH-nahr)—a device for detecting objects under water by reflection of sound waves

surveillance (suhr-VAY-lahns)—close watch kept over someone or something

ABOUT THE AUTHOR

Earle Rice Jr. is a former senior design engineer and technical writer in the aerospace, electronic-defense, and nuclear industries. He has devoted full time to his writing since 1993, and has specialized in military subjects. Earle is the author of more than ninety published books. He is listed in *Who's Who in America* and is a member of the Society of Children's Book Writers and Illustrators, the League of World War I Aviation Historians, the Air Force Association, and the Disabled American Veterans.